PLACES AND PEOPLE

China

Julia Waterlow

Franklin Watts
A Division of Grolier Publishing
New York • London • Hong Kong • Sydney
Danbury, Connecticut

A Division of Grolier Publishing
Sherman Turnpike
Danbury, Connecticut 06816

10 9 8 7 6 5 4 3 2 1

Library of Congress Cataloging-in-Publication Data

Waterlow, Julia.
China / Julia Waterlow.
p. cm. — (Places and people)
Summary: Examines the way in which China's geography has influenced its social, economic, and political structure.
Includes index.
ISBN 0-531-14271-X
1. China—Juvenile literature. [1. China - Civilization.
2. Human geography.] 1. Title. II. Series.
II. Series.
DS706.W333 1994
951 - dc20 93-20428
CIP AC

First paperback edition published
in 1996 by Franklin Watts

ISBN 0-531-15290-1

Series consultant: Anna Sanderman
Editor: Jane Walker
Design: Ron Kamen, Green Door Design Ltd
Cover design: Mike Davis
Maps: Mainline Design
Visual Image
Additional artwork: Mainline Design
Visual Image
Cover artwork: Raymond Turvey
Fact checking: Simone K. Lefolii

Cover photographs: left, The Great Wall of China (Julia Waterlow); middle, "Building our new Great Wall" poster displayed in Chengdu (Julia Waterlow); right, Storage jars being transported in Qufu (Julia Waterlow).

Photographic credits (t = top, m = middle, b = bottom): J. Eye Ubiquitous 17(b) Julia Waterlow, 25(b) L. Fordyce, 27 (m) Matthew McKee.
All other photographs supplied by Julia Waterlow.

Printed in Belgium

Contents

The Middle Kingdom

For centuries China has been hidden from the rest of the world by barriers of mountains and sea. The ancient Chinese cared little about what lay beyond their land. They believed that China was at the center of all civilization; even now they call China the "Middle Kingdom." For outsiders, it is one of the least known and understood countries in the world.

This secretive giant is the world's third largest country in terms of land area. It also has the largest population of any nation on earth. Despite its size, about half of China's land is uninhabitable so its huge population has to survive on the relatively small amount of land that can be used. Cities and farmland are crowded, and China only just manages to feed and house all its people.

China lies in Asia and has its longest borders with Russia, Mongolia, and India. It faces out toward the Pacific Ocean.

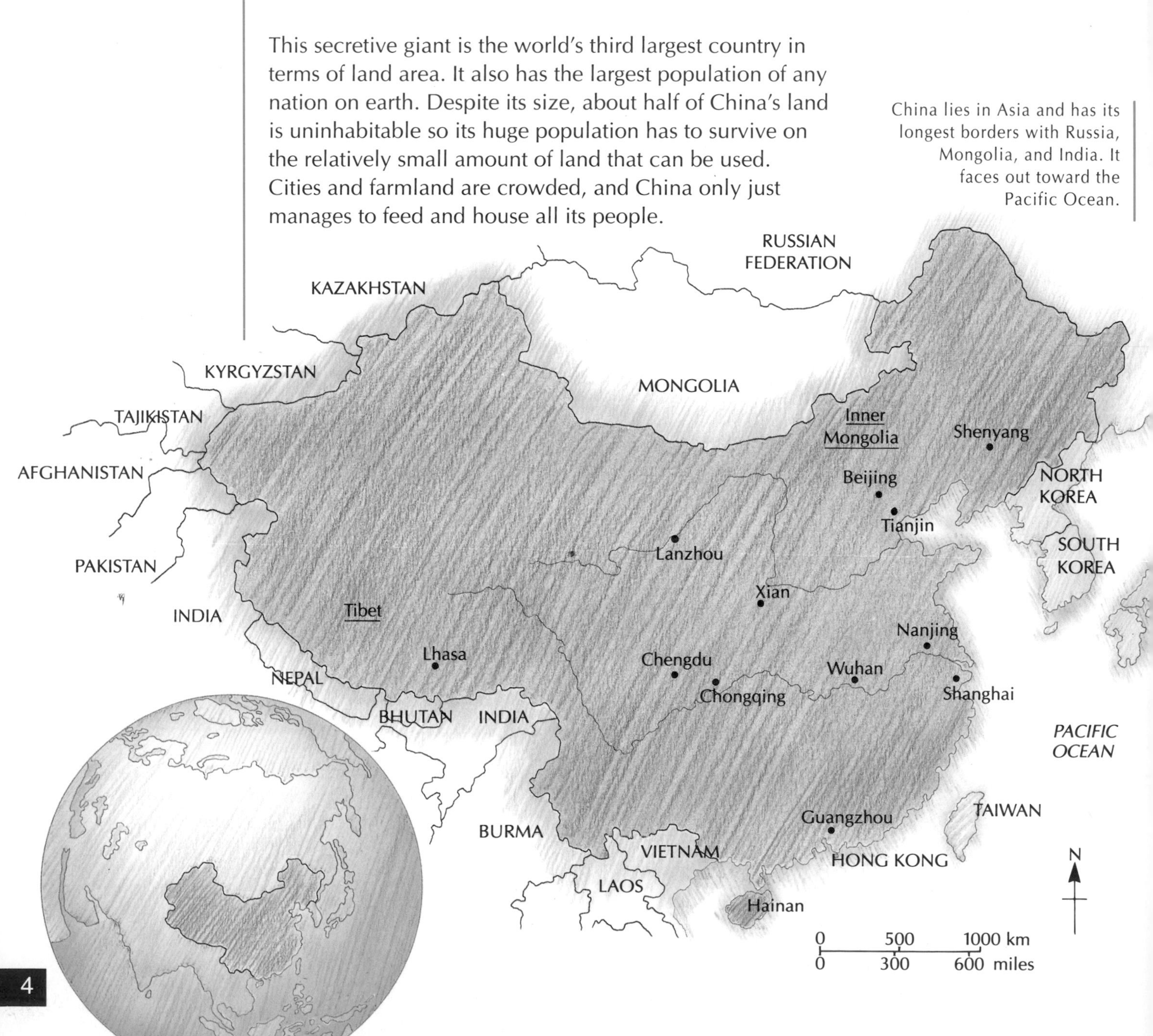

Life for people in the countryside is very different from life for those in the big cities of China. Little has changed over centuries in China's villages, whereas the cities are fast becoming like those in any modern country.

China today

Over the past 100 years, China has seen political upheavals and revolution but today it is firmly controlled by a communist government. Although life for most Chinese people has improved during the past 40 years, China is still struggling as an underdeveloped country. Many areas remain backward and unmodernized. However, recent changes and freedoms have led to fast economic growth, and China could well develop into a leading world nation.

China is gradually opening up to the outside world, allowing in foreigners to travel and to do business. Outsiders now have a chance to see how China's people live, the problems the country faces, and how these are influenced by its geography.

Two thousand years ago, a Chinese emperor ordered workers to connect a number of existing walls to form one continuous wall across northern China. The Great Wall, thousands of miles long, would help to protect the country against invaders. China has natural safeguards of mountains and sea on other sides, but not to the north. The wall has been rebuilt and strengthened many times to keep China safe from outsiders.

A vast and varied land

China's huge area includes almost every imaginable kind of terrain and climate.

The high plateau

A large part of southwestern China consists of a high plateau that is broken up by mountain ranges. Because the plateau's average altitude is about 13,120 feet (4,000 m), it is sometimes called "the roof of the world." The rough land and cold climate of this region make it bleak, and much of it is uninhabited because it is difficult to grow crops. Nomads live here in tents and move with the seasons in search of fresh grazing land for their animals.

China is a huge country with many different landscapes.

Taklimakan Desert
Gobi Desert
KUNLAN SHAN
Lake Qinghai
Yellow River (Huang He)
TIBETAN PLATEAU
YELLOW SEA
HIMALAYAS
Yangtze River (Chang Jiang)
N
SOUTH CHINA SEA
0 500 1000 km
0 300 600 miles

rivers
desert
lowlands
loess lands
mountainous areas
Sichuan Basin

Lowland areas

From the mountains, rivers flow down to plains in the east of China and then out into the Yellow Sea and the East China Sea. Most people live on these flatter areas, especially around the two valleys of the great rivers, the Yellow River and the Yangtze River (called the Huang He and Chang Jiang in Chinese). The region has rich soil and a good water supply.

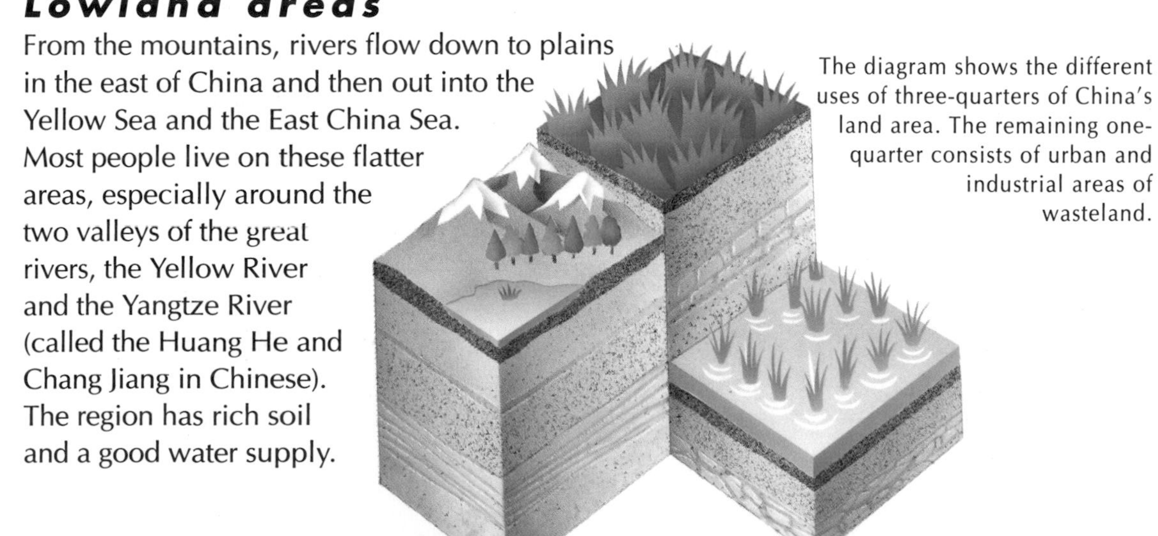

The diagram shows the different uses of three-quarters of China's land area. The remaining one-quarter consists of urban and industrial areas of wasteland.

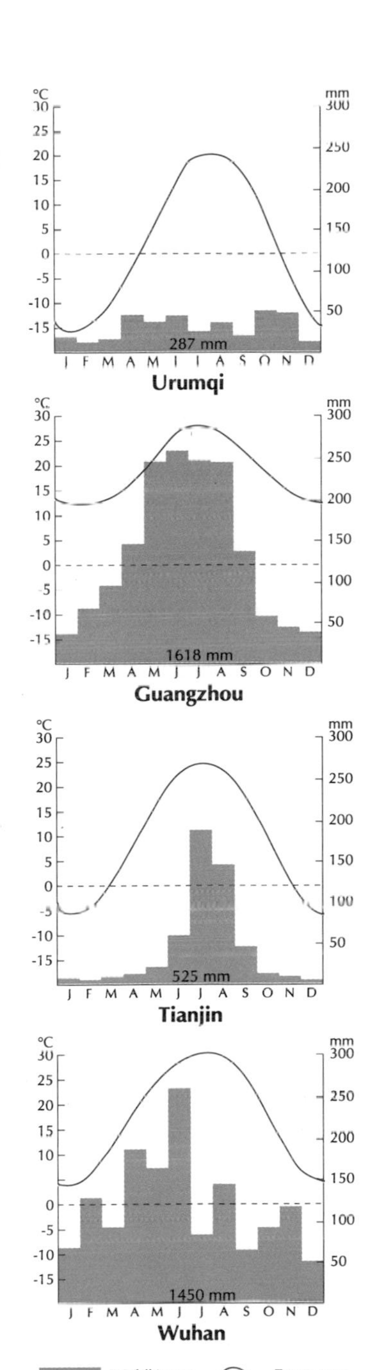

The graph shows the annual temperature and rainfall in four different Chinese cities. China's climate changes from freezing cold winters and hot summers in the north, to tropical and warm all year round on the south coast.

The Sichuan Basin is a rich farming region surrounded by mountains, lying roughly in the middle of China. Its name, meaning "four rivers," refers to the rivers that flow across the area, providing water and fertile soil. The basin and its surrounding area make up one of the most populated areas in the country. To the west huge mountains rise on the edge of Tibet, so most of the people live in the eastern half of the area.

To the south

Southern China is not as flat as the northern part of the country. It has a warm, wet climate which means that crops grow well during most of the year. The valleys are thickly populated and heavily farmed. Further to the southwest, the land becomes steeper and less easy to cultivate.

The south of China is warm and wet, providing plenty of water for crops like rice.

Deserts, oases, and loess

The rainfall is so low in much of northern China that there are large areas of desert. Along the old desert route between China and central Asia (called the Silk Road), oases watered by underground streams support farms and scattered towns.

The soft loess is easily eroded by wind and rain, creating steep-sided gullies. Many trees have been planted to reduce the soil erosion.

Part of northeast China is covered by a fine yellow-colored soil called loess. Although this area is still a rich and fertile farming region, in places the landscape is dry and dusty. Occasional heavy rains often sweep away fields, causing landslides. Huge amounts of loess are carried into the Yellow River, making it like a thick, muddy, yellow soup.

The people of China

Han Chinese women with their babies.

China's population totals nearly 1,200 million (that is 1,200,000,000) people. This means that around one in every five people on our planet is Chinese. Most are "Han" Chinese, who are the original Chinese from the Yellow River valley where Chinese civilization began about 4,000 years ago. They are called Han Chinese after one of China's great dynasties, the Han Dynasty (206 B.C. – A.D. 220).

As their civilization developed, the Han Chinese spread out along the Yellow and Yangtze river valleys and the population grew. As they moved into border areas to expand their territory, the Han Chinese came into contact with people of different races, and in some places took over their land. Today more than 90 million people (over 8 percent of the population) living in China are not Han Chinese.

Religion is strongest in China's minority areas. These people at Samye monastery in Tibet are celebrating the Tibetan full moon festival.

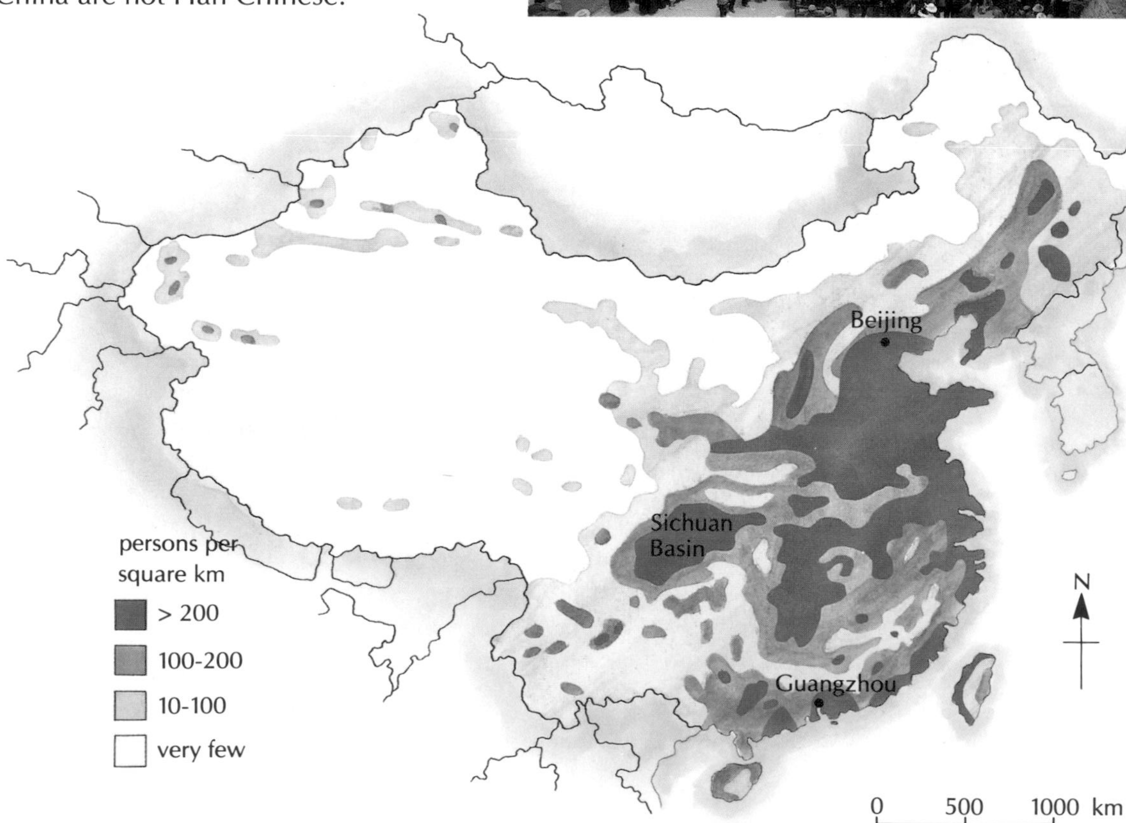

Population density in China. The map shows how China's population is concentrated in the eastern half of the country.

China's minorities

There are around 55 groups of non-Han Chinese living in China. They are called "China's minorities" and include people like the Tibetans and Mongolians, the Zhuang and the Miao. Most of these people have been forced to adopt Chinese ways of life, dress, and attitude. Some proudly try to keep their own traditions and religions alive. Han Chinese often look down on the minorities, believing them to be uncivilized and backward.

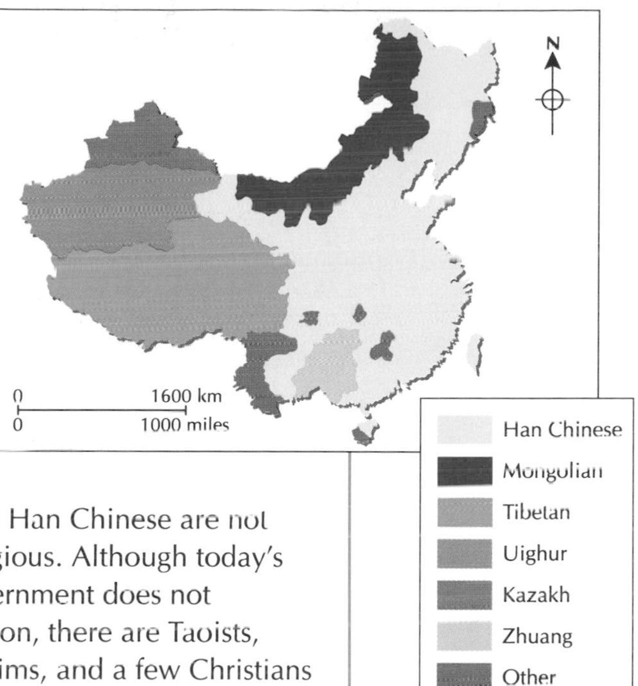

The areas occupied by the Han Chinese and by China's largest minority groups.

A family of Hui Muslims in Lanzhou celebrates the end of Ramadan, the month of fasting.

Traditionally the Han Chinese are not particularly religious. Although today's communist government does not encourage religion, there are Taoists, Buddhists, Muslims, and a few Christians who are allowed to worship. China has over 12 million Muslims, who for many generations have followed the Islamic religion brought to China by Arab traders and soldiers hundreds of years before. The majority live in the northwestern provinces. Some are of Turkish origin and do not look much like the Chinese.

Language and writing

Official government policy in China says that everyone should learn to speak and write Chinese. Even the minorities, many of whom have their own language and writing, are expected to learn Chinese. Learning Chinese characters (a character is a written word in Chinese) is hard work because there is no alphabet and each character's meaning and pronunciation have to be learned by heart. Out of about 50,000 characters, most Chinese know about 5,000, which is enough to read a newspaper.

A letter writer outside a post office helps people who have to write difficult formal letters. Each Chinese character is made up of a number of brush or pen lines and represents one word. The meaning of a character is always fixed, but the way it is pronounced varies with different dialects.

Farming and food

Chinese farming is based on growing crops, not raising animals. Land that is planted with crops produces more food than would be provided by keeping animals on the same amount of land – and China has a huge population to feed. Large numbers of animals are raised only in those parts of the country where it is impossible to grow crops. Although the Chinese like to eat meat, it is not an everyday part of many people's diet.

The map shows the main agricultural uses of China's land. The dotted line represents the lowest average annual temperature (7°F/4°C), so areas south of the line are unlikely to get frosts. The solid line represents average annual rainfall. South of the line it is warm and wet, so rice can be grown. To the north the weather is much drier and cold in winter and so wheat is planted.

Mongolia and Northwest
Mainly pasture and grazing sheep, goats, horses and cattle on open steppe. Cold winters. Turns to desert in the west.

North China Plain and Yellow River Valley
Mainly wheat. Too cold and not wet enough for rice. Also millet, kaoliang, cotton and corn.

Northeast
Cold northern winter gives only short growing season: soya beans, kaoliang and corn.

Yangtze Valley
Wheat in winter, rice in summer. Also cotton.

Oases of Northwest
In dry desert regions farming only in oases, using underground water pumped into fields.

South of Yangtze
Rice is staple crop because warm all year round. Also tea and silk.

Tibetan Plateau
High-altitude rough pasture. Sheep and yaks. Barley grown in sheltered areas.

7°F/4°C

1000mm 39 in {rainfall

South China
Wet tropical climate allows at least two crops of rice per year. Wide variety of fruits.

Southwest
Hilly region. Rice is main crop. Mixture of other crops, mainly grown on terraced hillsides.

Sichuan Basin
Wheat and rice. Climate allows long growing season so many other crops, e.g. cotton, sugar cane and tobacco.

N

0 2000 km
0 1250 miles

Throughout China, families have their own small vegetable patches beside their houses. Around the towns and cities there are larger vegetable fields where food is grown for the urban population. Many villages and towns have fish ponds. Fish is a valuable source of protein for those who cannot afford to eat meat regularly.

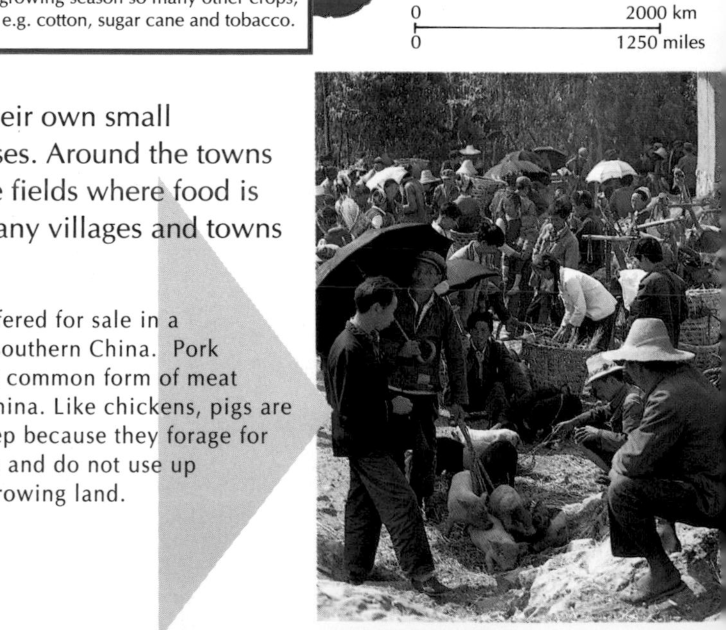

Pigs are offered for sale in a market in southern China. Pork is the most common form of meat eaten in China. Like chickens, pigs are easy to keep because they forage for themselves and do not use up valuable growing land.

FACT BOX

- China produces more of the following than any other country in the world: cotton, rice, sweet potatoes, onions, carrots, cucumbers, eggs, goat's meat, pigs, mules, horses.
- China is the world's biggest grower of watermelons.
- China produces more than one-third of the world's tobacco.
- China is the world's largest producer of rapeseed (for making oil).
- Over half the world's silk comes from China.

Farming methods

As so little land in China is suitable for growing crops, the Chinese have developed many ways of getting the best out of what they have. In order to grow more and better plants on land that has been used for years, they regularly use fertilizer, including "night soil" (human waste). Two or more crops may also be grown on one piece of land; for example, watermelons may be sown in between rows of cotton plants.

If possible, land is used all year round, as in central China where the spring wheat harvest is immediately followed by plowing, flooding the fields, and sowing rice for the summer. The Chinese have built hundreds of thousands of miles of irrigation channels so that even distant fields can be watered.

Most farm labor in China is still done by hand, although new techniques and better equipment have helped and many villages now have tractors. But in many places machines are not practical because the land is so hilly and because human labor is plentiful and much cheaper than mechanized forms.

Hillsides are made into useful farmland by cutting terraces, such as these rice ones in Guangxi.

A girl helps her mother to pick tea. Most tea is grown on hillsides in the south and east of China. Although it is exported, a lot is produced for the home market too. Other important cash (commercial) crops in China are silk and cotton, which are used both for making textiles for use in China and for export abroad.

An organized society

Governing China is not easy because the country covers such a large area and has such a huge population. China is not a democratic country and does not have general elections. The Communist Party, which came to power in 1949, holds the country together through a strong central system and strict control over Chinese people's lives.

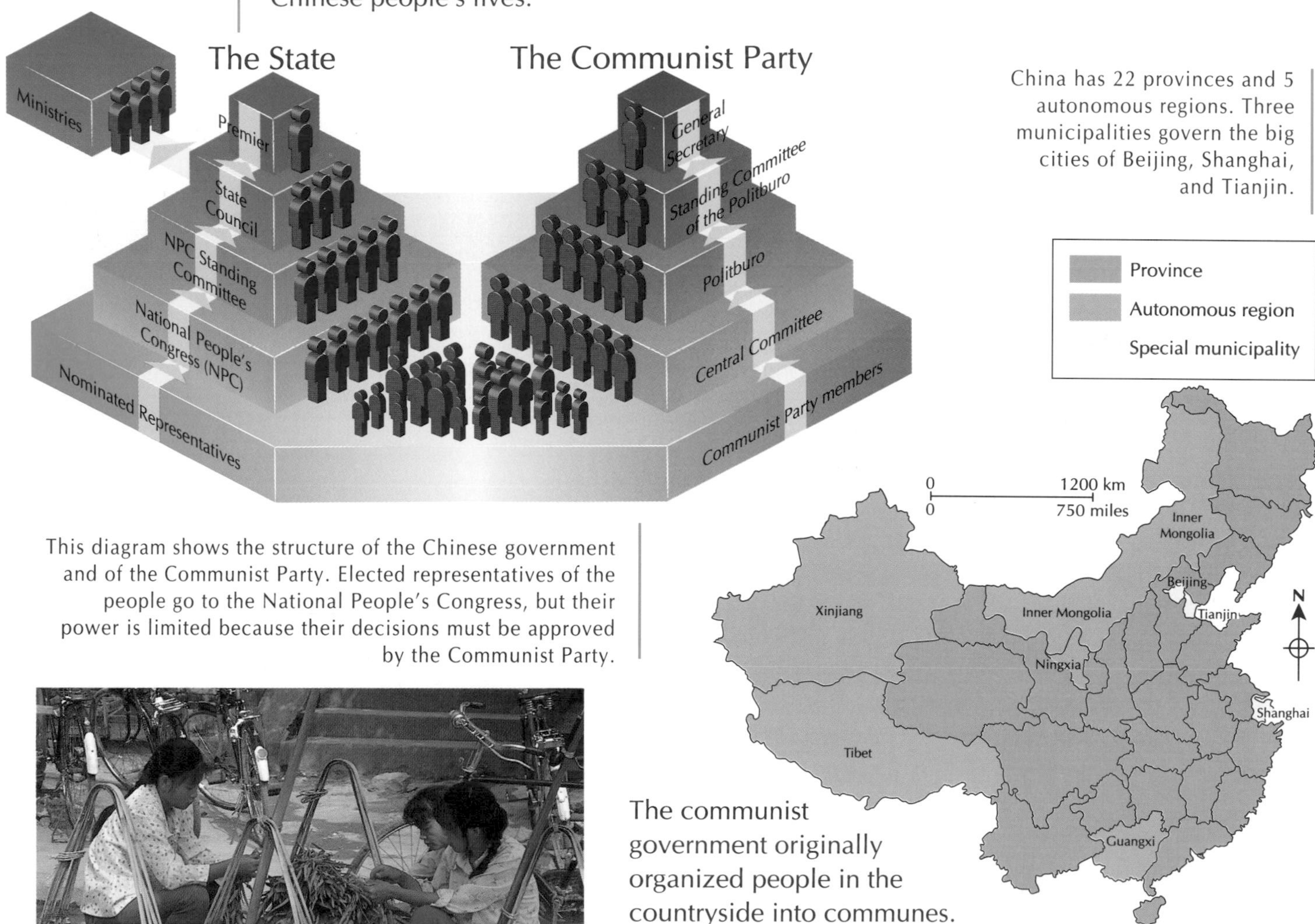

China has 22 provinces and 5 autonomous regions. Three municipalities govern the big cities of Beijing, Shanghai, and Tianjin.

This diagram shows the structure of the Chinese government and of the Communist Party. Elected representatives of the people go to the National People's Congress, but their power is limited because their decisions must be approved by the Communist Party.

Farmers have flocked to markets to sell their surplus produce since the Communist Party began to relax its control over the economy.

The communist government originally organized people in the countryside into communes. Groups of people (usually villages) would work together on communal land to grow what they were told was needed. They would later be given a share of the results. In order to encourage people to produce more, over the past 10 years the "responsibility system" has been introduced. Farmers now lease their land and make a contract with the government to supply a certain amount of produce. They can then grow whatever other crops they want, and sell the produce on the open market.

The Li family live in a two-bedroom apartment which is provided by the school where Mrs. Li works. Factories and other organizations, such as schools or the railroad company, are called "work units." Nearly everyone in China belongs to a work unit, which provides not only a job, but also housing, schools, hospitals, and facilities for sports and recreation.

Control over work

Industry and business too were owned and controlled by the government. Although people are now allowed to run their own businesses, most still work for state-run companies. In the past, these companies guaranteed people's wages and jobs for life. This system is called the "iron rice bowl" because it ensured that people would never be short of food. Since 1984, however, new employees have been given a job contract for a fixed number of years.

Chinese people can seldom choose the job they do, even if they are well qualified. The government regulates and controls jobs and housing. Everyone has to carry an identity card showing their place of work and where they live. Until recently, it was impossible even to travel to another city without permission.

Mao Zedong led the Communist Party to power in 1949 and remained China's leader until he died in 1976.

Education

The government has tried to ensure that everyone receives some education. In 1949 only one in five people could read and write, but now the majority of people have these basic skills. However, for young people anywhere in China, the chances of going on to higher education after school are very limited.

There is a shortage of schools, teachers, and equipment, particularly in the rural areas, where few children attend school beyond primary level.

Natural hazards

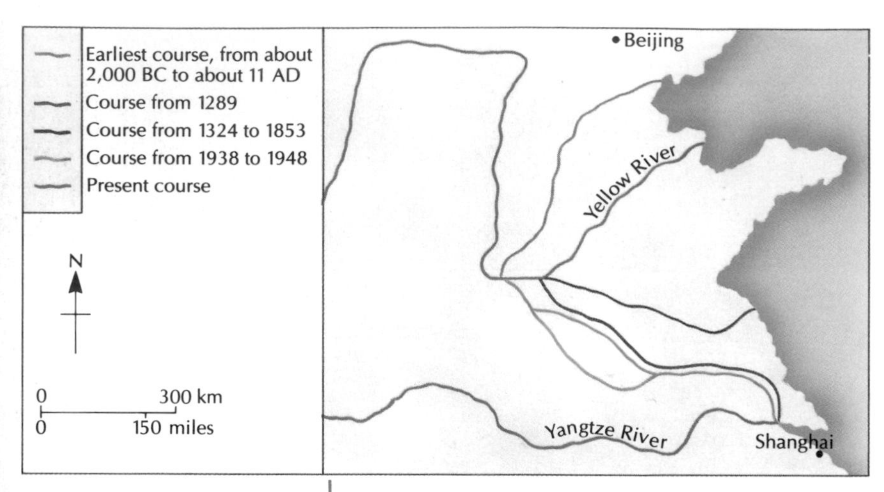

When the Yellow River broke its banks, it sometimes changed its course completely. It swung as much as 500 miles (800 km) from north to south, devastating homes and crops.

Throughout its long history China has suffered from the effects of natural hazards such as floods, droughts, and earthquakes. The Yellow River and Yangtze River have overflowed many times, destroying homes and farmland. Rains have failed for months on end, leaving crops dying, and sudden earth tremors have caused landslides, resulting in the collapse of buildings.

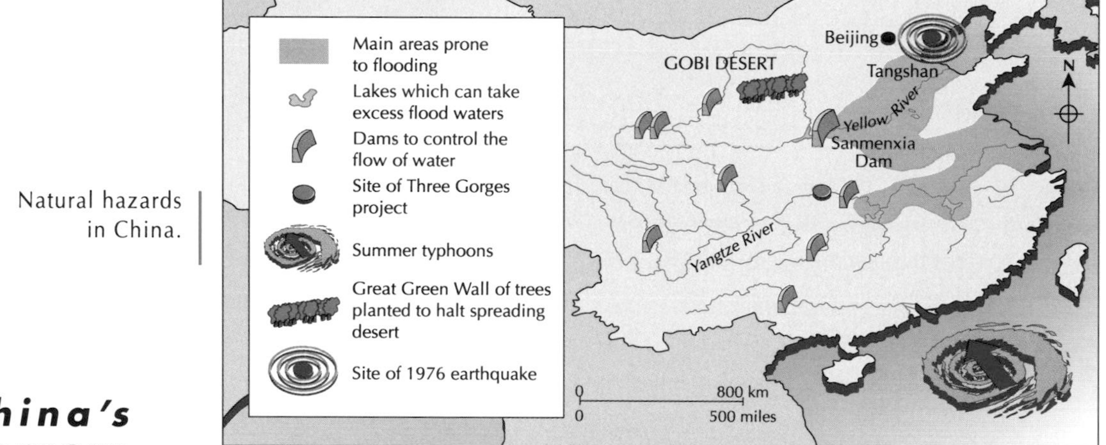

Natural hazards in China.

China's sorrow

Yellow River floods have caused more deaths than any other river floods in the world – the river has been nicknamed "China's sorrow." Loess soil is carried downstream by the river and deposited on the northern plains of China. As a result, the riverbed here lies high above the level of the surrounding land.

Water control

The Chinese put a huge effort into tackling one of their main problems – water control. For centuries China's vast workforce has been used to tame the country's rivers by strengthening banks and building flood diversion channels. Today, modern techniques like dam building are also important.

If the Yellow River's protective dikes break, it is almost impossible to stop water from streaming out over the countryside from and causing a major disaster.

Work on the San-men-hsia Dam began in the 1950s to control the Yellow River's frequent flooding and to provide hydroelectric power. However, within a few years the dam was blocked by the vast quantities of silt brought down by the Yellow River, and it had to be modified. Even though the dam now helps to stop major floods lower down the Yellow River, it only produces a fraction of the hydroelectric power expected. The Three Gorges Dam project along the Yangtze River is one of the largest dam schemes ever proposed in the world.

Silt continues to fill up the reservoir behind the San-men-hsia Dam. It could block up the dam again within the next 50 years.

As well as controlling rivers to prevent floods, dams also provide a reservoir of water which can be used when there is a drought. This is particularly important in northern China where rainfall is unreliable. China's huge population needs more and more water, for both home and industry, and there are sometimes water shortages in the northern cities.

This poster relates the events of the earthquake that struck the coal-mining city of Tangshan in July 1976. About 250,000 people died, 165,000 were badly injured, and most of the city's buildings were damaged or destroyed.

The Great Green Wall

Deserts in the north of China are being blown south and are advancing on inhabited areas. A belt of trees, called the Great Green Wall, hundreds of miles long, has been planted on the desert edges to protect towns and farmland. Trees and terraces are being used in the loess area to hold the soft soil in place and to prevent erosion.

Part of the Great Green Wall shown here is preventing the desert from advancing on the town of Dingbian in northern China.

Resources and power

China is the third largest producer of energy in the world and has vast resources. In China's growing economy the demand for power from industries and households is rapidly increasing, but getting power to the user is often difficult. Many energy resources are far from where the power is needed, and as a result there are energy shortages in many areas.

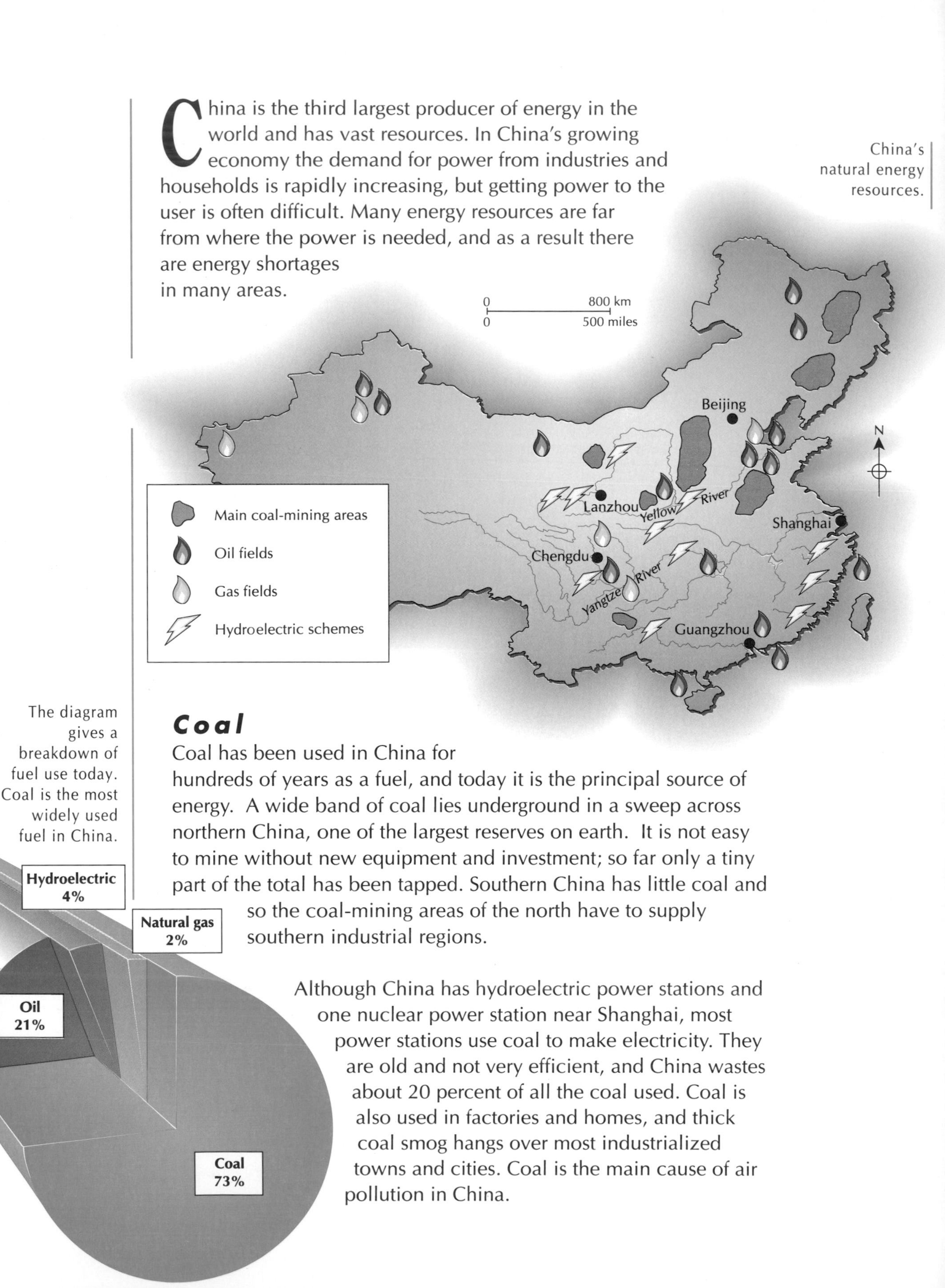

China's natural energy resources.

The diagram gives a breakdown of fuel use today. Coal is the most widely used fuel in China.

Coal

Coal has been used in China for hundreds of years as a fuel, and today it is the principal source of energy. A wide band of coal lies underground in a sweep across northern China, one of the largest reserves on earth. It is not easy to mine without new equipment and investment; so far only a tiny part of the total has been tapped. Southern China has little coal and so the coal-mining areas of the north have to supply southern industrial regions.

Although China has hydroelectric power stations and one nuclear power station near Shanghai, most power stations use coal to make electricity. They are old and not very efficient, and China wastes about 20 percent of all the coal used. Coal is also used in factories and homes, and thick coal smog hangs over most industrialized towns and cities. Coal is the main cause of air pollution in China.

Hydroelectric power

Hydroelectricity could become an important source of energy, for China has many large and powerful rivers. The problem is that few suitable sites for damming rivers lie near the centers of population. One example of a difficult location is the fast-flowing upper reaches of the Yellow River, high in the mountains to the west. It is both difficult and expensive to bring electricity to the cities from this remote region.

Restaurants pile up the coal they use on the pavement outside. They use coal for cooking because electricity is too expensive and there is little gas available.

Oil and gas

Oil has been discovered in several areas of China, many of them in remote inland regions. China uses some of the oil for its own needs and also exports it. Oil found in the deserts of the northwest is brought by pipeline to the town of Lanzhou, which has refineries to process it. China's biggest gas fields are found in the Sichuan Basin. The gas is used to power local industries and as a fuel for running buses.

Solar energy is being used here to heat up water in the kettle.

Local energy

The Chinese also produce energy on a small scale, for home or village use. In the countryside, where fuel like wood is scarce and coal is too expensive, methane or biogas is used as fuel. It is made by letting human, animal, and crop waste rot and ferment in a tank.

In some areas, like Inner Mongolia, wind generators have been successful in producing household electricity. In sunny areas, particularly at high altitude, solar power is used on a small scale for heating water.

Industry and business

It was not until after 1949 that China started industrial development in earnest. The country concentrated on heavy industries, producing materials like steel and manufacturing machines. These industries are still vital because China needs raw materials and machinery to supply its new and growing industries. As well as coal, China has its own rich reserves of other minerals, particularly iron, and so little needs to be imported.

China's main industrial areas and the location of its Special Economic Zones.

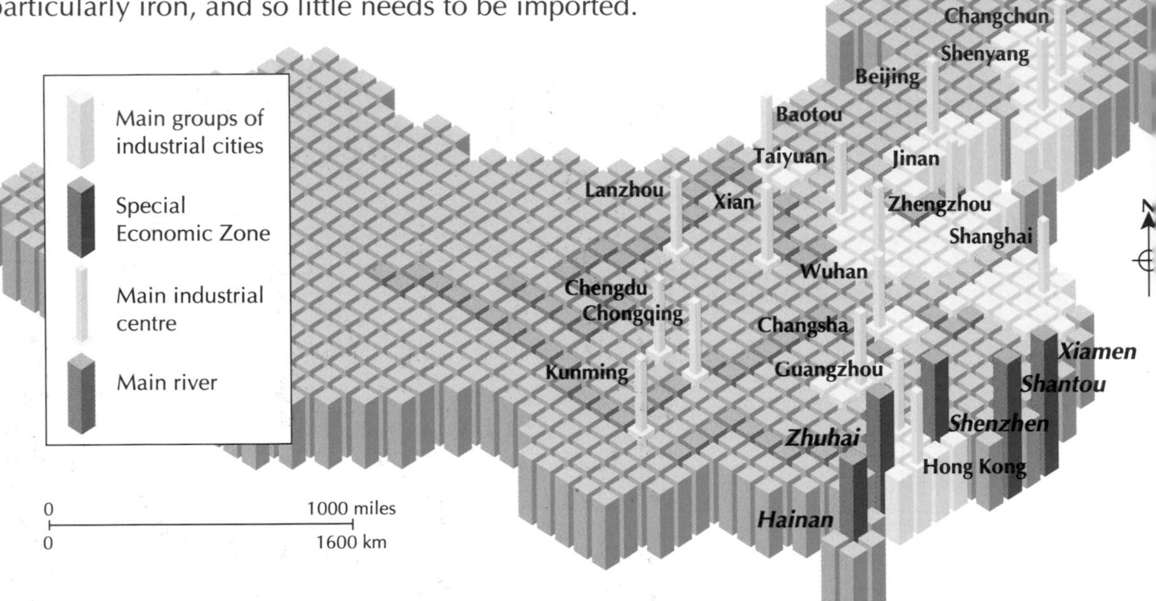

The main areas of heavy industry lie near these natural resources, as in the northeast where both coal and iron are found. Around the iron and steel factories are engineering plants producing machinery and equipment which are sent all over China.

Special Economic Zones

Along the coast, special areas have been created where foreign companies can set up joint businesses with the Chinese. These areas are known as Special Economic Zones, or SEZs for short. The foreign companies benefit by using cheap Chinese labor and materials, and the Chinese receive foreign currency in return. High-tech companies are encouraged so that China has a chance to learn about modern equipment and processes.

New freedoms in China have resulted in private businesses being set up. By 1990 over 8 million had been created. A wide choice of goods is for sale, and stores and markets have a brisk trade.

The big cities

Other industrial areas have grown up where there are large numbers of people and good communications. The regions around the big cities of Beijing, Tianjin, and Shanghai have long been the wealthiest trading and business centers of China. Although the government has tried to encourage industry in more backward areas of the country, the greatest growth has continued to be in the heavily populated regions nearer the coast.

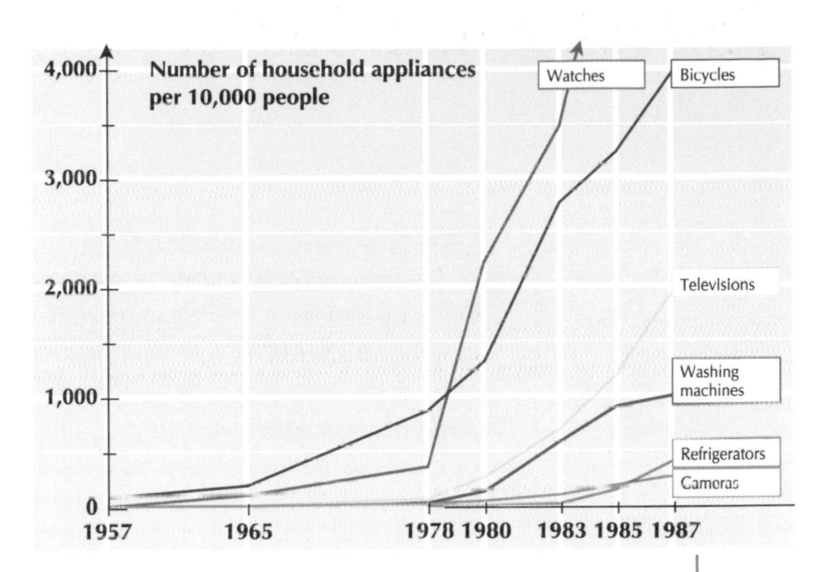

The graph shows the growth in the ownership of household appliances. There has been a big boom in consumer goods as Chinese people have more money to spend.

The towns in the Shanghai region, for example, have a wide variety of industries and businesses including shipbuilding, chemical manufacturing, cotton and silk factories as well as companies making consumer goods like radios, watches, and cameras. Most of these things are made for the Chinese market.

A man makes steel rods by melting down old railroad tracks. This is a typical business set up to make goods for local use.

All Chinese towns and cities have industries processing local products, such as canning factories that pack locally grown fruit, or mills that spin wool from sheep. Towns often make bricks or cement for their own building needs and manufacture some light goods to supply the growing consumer markets. The government encourages small, light industries at village or township level, producing goods needed locally and some to be sold elsewhere in China. These industries help to employ people in rural areas and improve the local economy.

Problems

Industry in China has many problems. Factories are mostly old with outdated machinery and their products are often poorly made. Improvements are held up by a shortage of skilled people and also by difficulties in obtaining new equipment. Chinese industry suffers too because of problems with the supply of power and raw materials.

Cement factories like this one in Mongolia are found in every province in China. As both the population and business grow, more and more buildings are needed.

Covering distances

Steam trains are still used in China, particularly in the north where there is plenty of coal for fuel. New trains in China are now diesel or electric.

China's size and rough terrain make traveling a slow business. The country's size alone means that over 600,000 miles (1 million km) of roads and railroads have had to be built. The large areas of mountainous and hilly land, and the harsh climate, add to the difficulties posed by the size of China's land area.

By rail

Railroads are the main method of transporting goods and people over the vast distances. Trains are not the fastest way to travel, but they carry bulky goods and large numbers of people both cheaply and easily.

Most of the early railroad lines were built by foreign companies and served mainly coastal regions, but the communist government extended lines far into China to help inland areas. Today's expanding economy and rising population have put a great strain on the railroad network, which is neither modern nor large enough to cope. Delays cause problems for industry and business all over China.

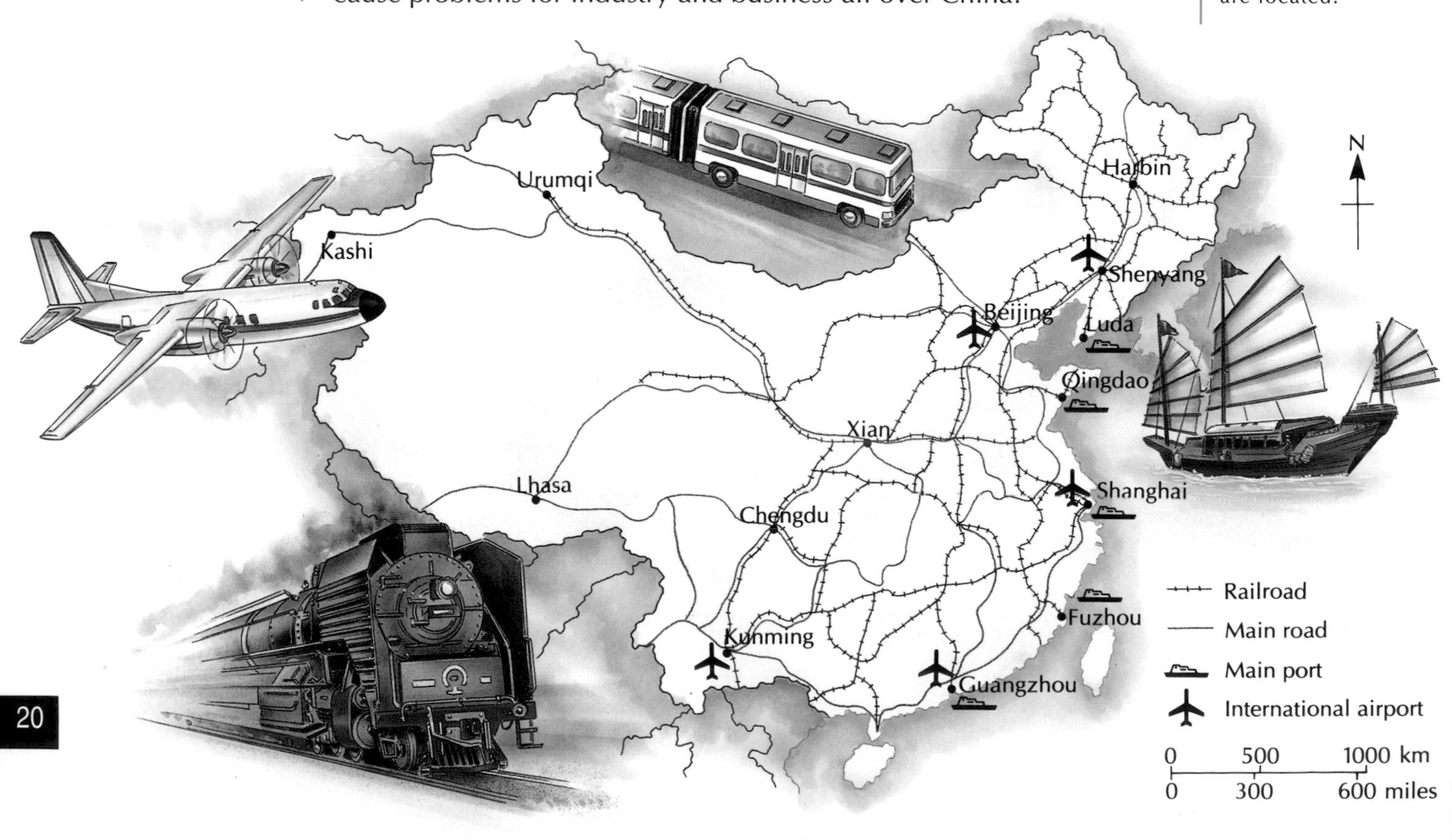

The map shows China's transport network. The main transport routes are in the east because that is where most people and industries are located.

Transport by water

Canals and rivers have always been important ways of moving goods around China, particularly in the south. The Yellow River is not used much because the water levels vary so greatly with the uncertain rainfall. The Yangtze and other rivers to the south can be used all year; the Yangtze has ports all along its length as far as Sichuan Province. China's coast has harbors too. These are becoming increasingly important with the growth of China's international trade.

A bicycle park in Kaifeng in central China. For local journeys the bicycle is the most common means of transportation. Today most families in China have bicycles, in the same way that families in developed countries have cars.

China's roads

People traveling between towns or villages take a train, boat, or bus because hardly anyone owns a car. Buses serve even remote villages in China. The roads in these rural areas are sometimes in terrible condition.

Main roads in the mountainous west of China are often washed away or blocked by landslides like this.

In much of China people have to carry things themselves or use animals, because they cannot afford any other means of transportation.

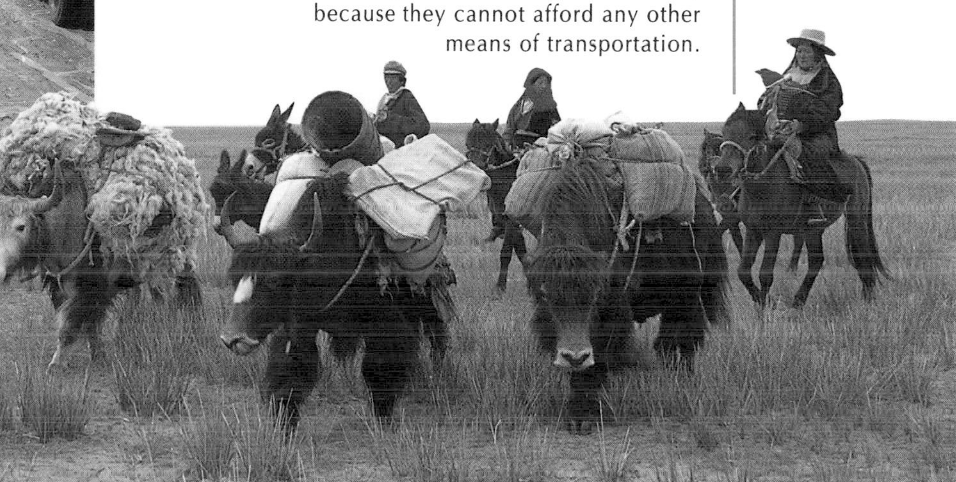

Roads nearer cities are better but they are often congested with taxis, buses, and trucks. The roads cannot handle the vast number of people and goods moving around the country. Air traffic is on the rise too, and most major cities have an airport.

Crowded cities

The Chinese have always built great cities. About 1,300 years ago Xian, then the capital of China, was the biggest city in the world. However, until recently, most Chinese lived in the countryside. It is only over the past 50 years that the urban population has really begun to grow. As industry developed, cities and towns expanded outward, with vast suburbs being built over surrounding farmland. Now there are about 40 cities with a population of over one million people.

Beijing

Beijing was China's capital under the foreign rule of the Mongols. Most of the succeeding Chinese dynasties kept it as their capital, and today it is the center of administration for the whole country. Beijing is laid out in a grid pattern and used to be surrounded by walls, as were many of China's cities. Although new residential and industrial suburbs are sprouting up around the city, and much of the center is being redeveloped with modern office complexes and hotels, the old single-story residential areas remain in the middle of Beijing.

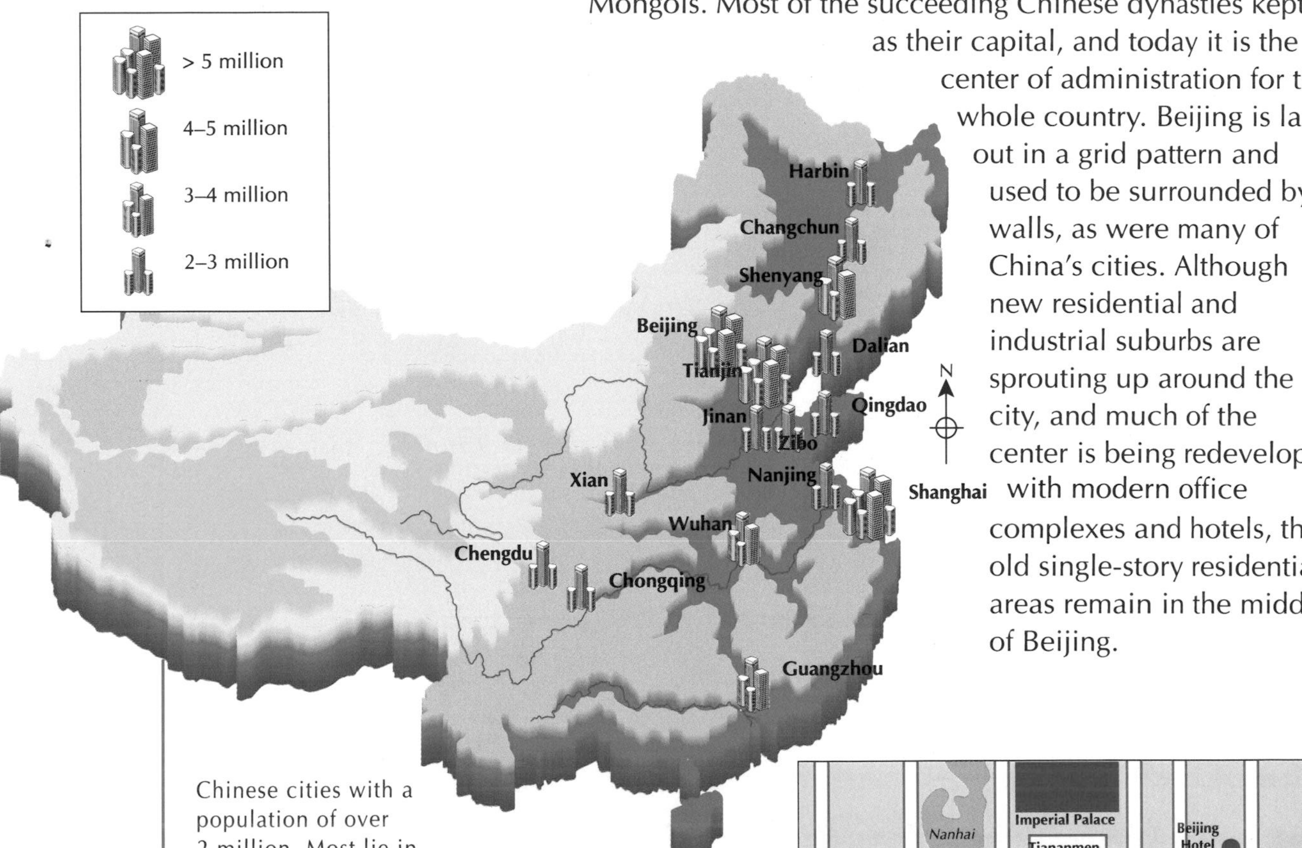

Chinese cities with a population of over 2 million. Most lie in the east of the country.

The streets of Beijing are laid out in a gridlike pattern.

eople from rural areas have been ding in thousands to the cities, in hope of finding well-paid work. ities already have unemployment and this influx will add to the problem.

Most capital cities in the world have a famous square or central area, and in Beijing it is Tiananmen Square. Parades and celebrations are held here. It is also where, in 1989, protesting Chinese students were shot by Chinese government soldiers.

Tiananmen Square lies in front of the main gate (Tiananmen) of the Imperial City. Within the Imperial City lies the "Forbidden City," which used to be the palace of the emperors of China. Ordinary citizens were forbidden from entering it, but today anyone can visit as a tourist.

Shanghai is one of the biggest and most crowded cities in the world. Its services, such as water, sewage, and power, are serving a population that is 10 times greater than the one for which they were designed.

Shanghai

Shanghai's growth dates from the nineteenth century when it was chosen by foreign powers to become their main base in China. It lies in a large agricultural region, has transportation links with cities up the Yangtze River, and is an important port for overseas trade. The city is one of China's leading manufacturing and business centers. With the largest urban population in China and its historical connections with the outside world, Shanghai leads the country in fashion and new ideas.

Guangzhou

Like Shanghai, Guangzhou has thrived due to foreign trade in the past. It continues to do so because it is so close to the international trading and financial center of Hong Kong. The farmland around Guangzhou supplies Hong Kong with much of its food. Business connections between the two cities have helped Guangzhou to set up modern and profitable factories, making it one of the richest cities in China.

Changing boundaries

China's long borders touch many other countries. Some, like the western border, are clearly marked by mountain ranges but others, like the one with Mongolia, are just political lines. There are also large areas within China's boundaries which are inhabited by people who are not Han Chinese. Many of these people are unhappy about Chinese control over what was once their own land. There is sometimes trouble and unrest in these areas.

Karakoram Pass along China's border with Pakistan. Mountains form the border between China and countries to the west, including Pakistan.

Tibet

Tibet is a huge mountain region that was once a separate country, although the Chinese had loose control over it for a while during part of the Qing dynasty (from 1720 onward). In 1959, the Chinese took control of Tibet by force. In the following years they destroyed the temples and monasteries of the religious Tibetans and imprisoned or killed those who resisted. New buildings and factories were built and the Tibetans were made to learn Chinese.

China's boundaries stretched out the furthest during the Qing dynasty (1644–1911), when the whole of Mongolia was part of China.

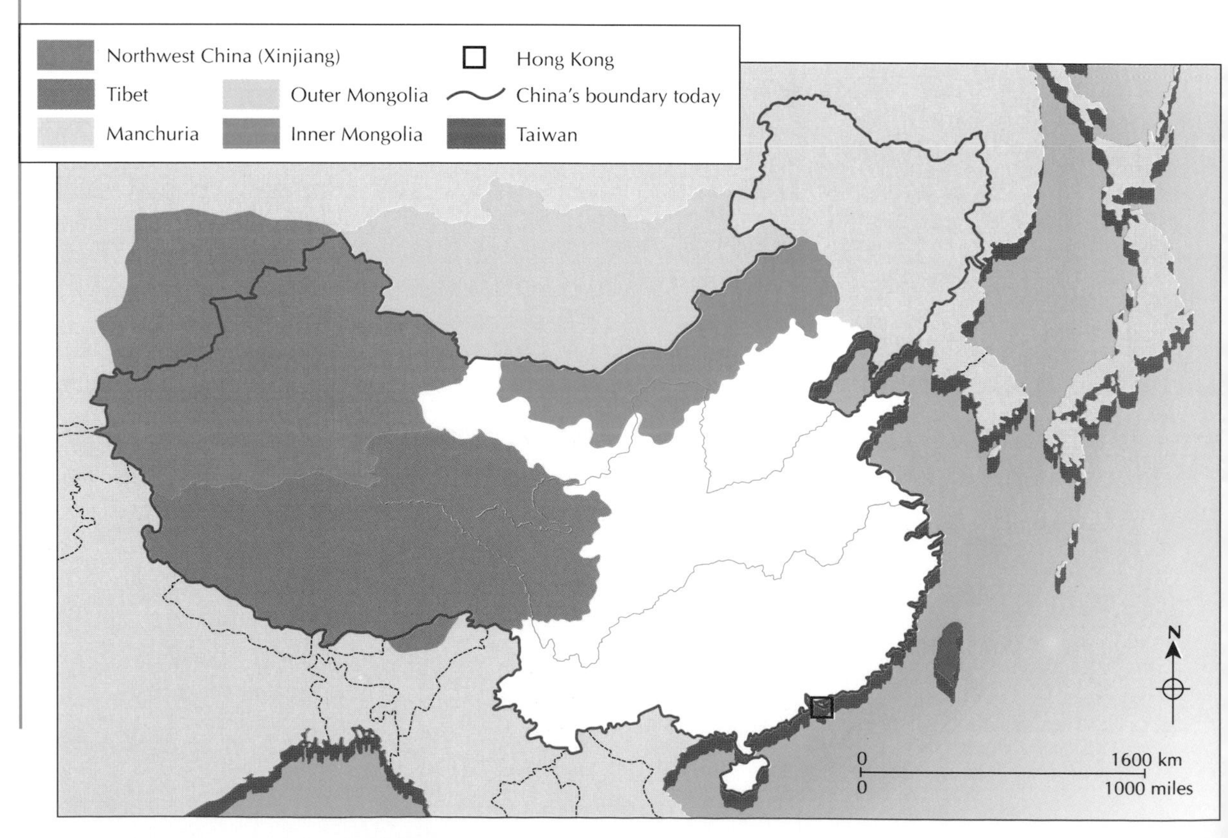

Muslims and Mongolians

Although it was never a separate state, the province called Xinjiang in the northwest only became a province of China during the Qing dynasty. The Muslim people who live here have fought the Chinese in the past, and in recent years there has been more unrest. One way in which the Chinese keep control here is to bring huge numbers of Han Chinese settlers into these remote parts of their empire. In Inner Mongolia, for example, the Han Chinese far outnumber the Mongolians.

Hong Kong is one of the world's main financial centers and a densely populated city region under British control. The British government has agreed to transfer control of Hong Kong to China in 1997. There are fears about how the communist government will treat the people of Hong Kong.

China and Mongolia have a long and intertwined history. In A.D. 1279 the Mongols invaded and ruled all China. During the Qing dynasty the Chinese controlled all Mongolia, but now only part of Mongolia lies inside China's borders (Inner Mongolia) and the rest is an independent country. Some Mongolians would like the country to be one.

The island of Taiwan has a mainly urban population and a successful modern economy. Taiwan and China have different governments but both claim to be the rightful government of both the Chinese mainland and Taiwan.

China and the outside world

For political reasons, in 1949 China's new communist government broke off contact with other countries, except for a few communist states such as the Soviet Union. The Soviet Union gave China a lot of help in building cities and developing its industries. Even though the two countries quarrelled in about 1960, there are many reminders in China today of its links with the Soviet Union. When China joined the United Nations in 1971, its cold relations with other noncommunist countries slowly began to thaw. The United States finally recognized the Chinese government in 1979.

The levels of imports and exports between China and its main trading partners. The value of foreign trade to the Chinese economy has nearly tripled in 10 years.

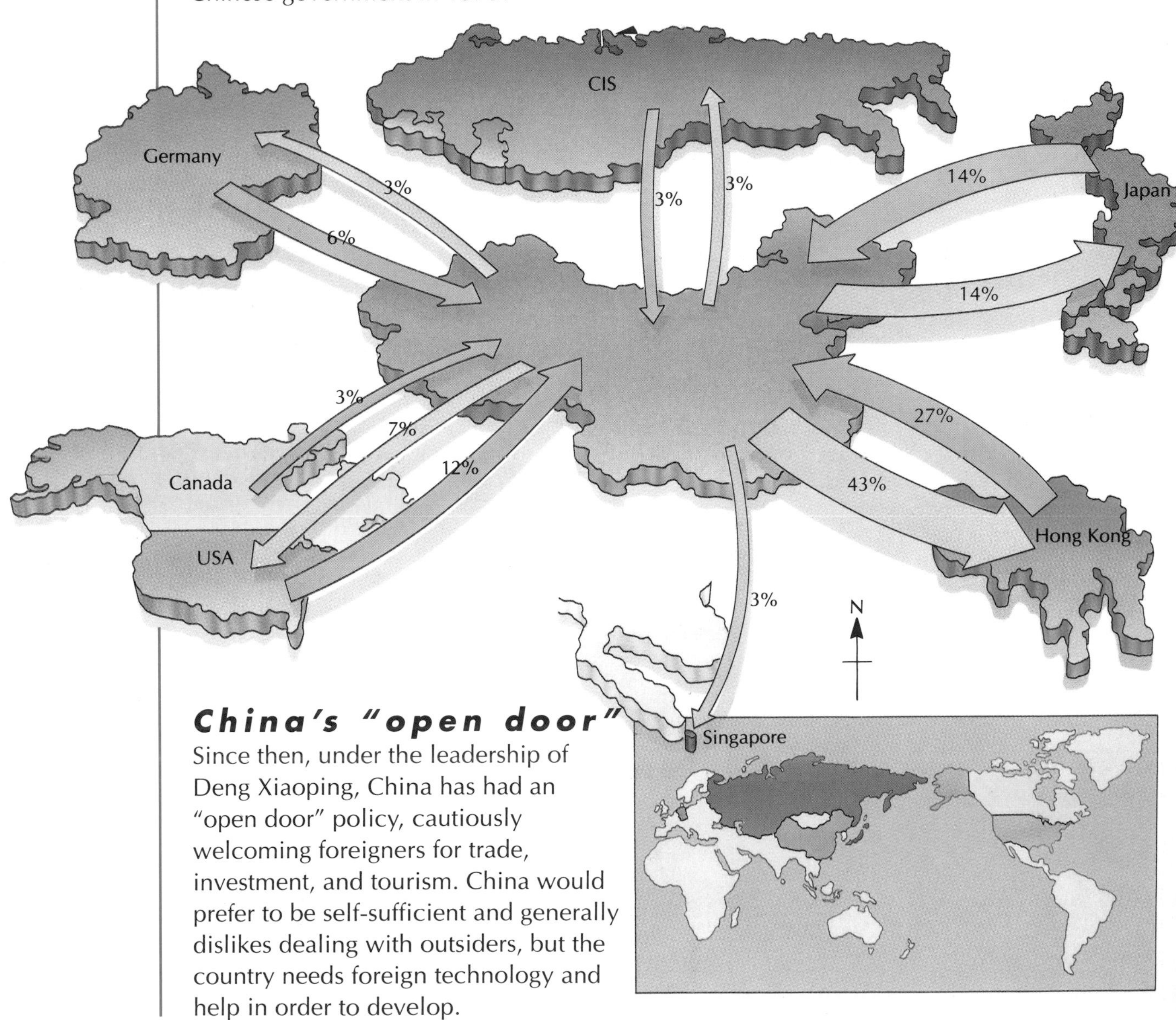

China's "open door"

Since then, under the leadership of Deng Xiaoping, China has had an "open door" policy, cautiously welcoming foreigners for trade, investment, and tourism. China would prefer to be self-sufficient and generally dislikes dealing with outsiders, but the country needs foreign technology and help in order to develop.

China's imports and exports. More and more finished goods, such as textiles, are produced for export. The main imports are modern machinery and equipment.

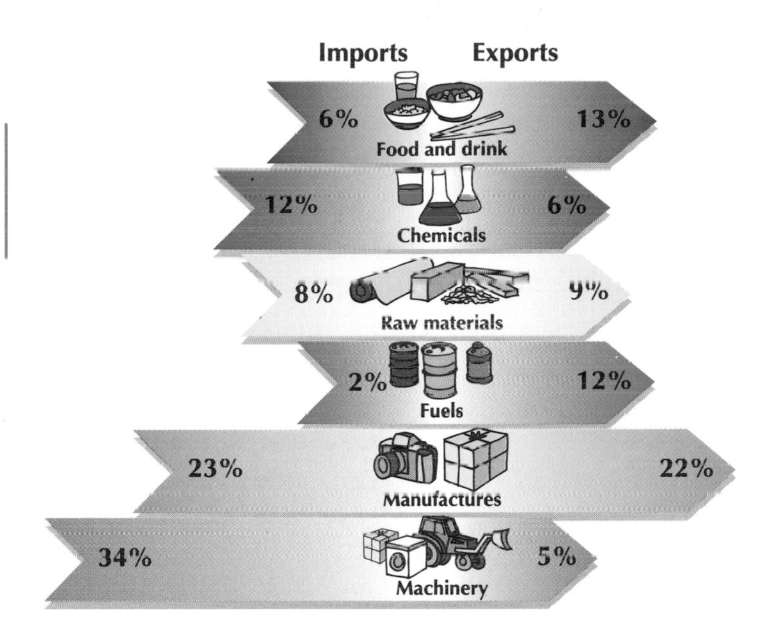

Since the 1980s foreign companies have been doing business with the Chinese. When government soldiers shot some of the protesting students in Tiananmen Square in 1989, many foreign countries were horrified and refused to continue trading with China. Business has picked up again now, but some foreigners are still concerned about political prisoners and human rights in China.

Foreign firms are anxious to do business in China because they can see a huge market for their products. When they sell equipment to China, they usually provide expert technical help and training as well, because the Chinese do not have the necessary knowledge. The Chinese like to keep control, however, and so projects for new factories or businesses are usually joint projects between a foreign and a Chinese company.

Companies like Volkswagen (a German firm that makes cars and buses) set up joint businesses to make their products in China.

Overseas Chinese

Over the past 100 years or so, many Chinese have left China because of civil war or because of desperate economic problems. Most come from the southeastern part of China. Although many overseas Chinese have settled in Asia, countries all over the world have Chinese communities.

Most capital cities around the world have a Chinese community. This is Chinatown in Sydney, Australia.

As China opens its doors to the outside world, more and more overseas Chinese are visiting China. They visit the town from which their family originally came because the Chinese like to honor their ancestors. Overseas Chinese are also involved in setting up successful businesses with mainland Chinese.

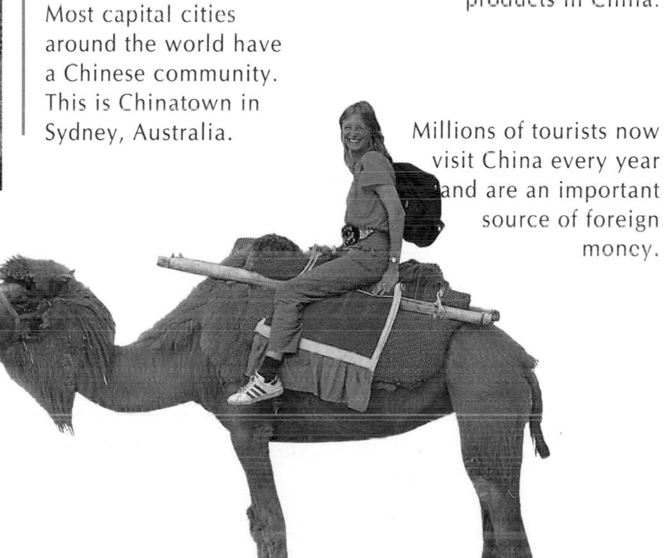

Millions of tourists now visit China every year and are an important source of foreign money.

Over 1.3 billion – the future

Birth control posters like this one often show female children to explain that girls are equal to boys.

China's huge and growing population is the main problem for the future. Since 1979, the government has attempted to restrict couples to having only one child, but still about 15 million babies are born every year. The aim is to keep the population below 1.3 billion by the year 2000. Despite the one-child campaign, there are reasons why China is unlikely to meet this target. Because food and health care are much improved, fewer children die and people live longer. The government has also been forced to relax its one-child policy in the countryside because it was so unpopular; rural families are now allowed to have two children.

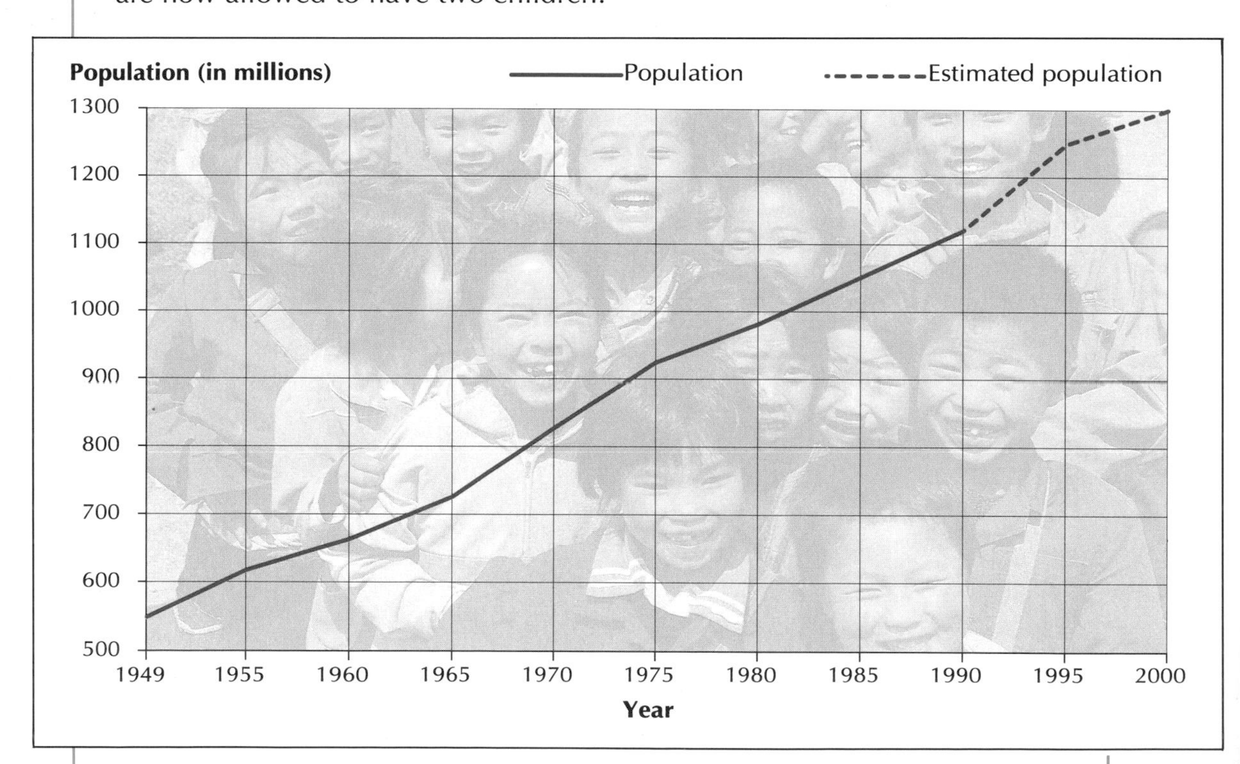

Population growth in China between 1949 and the year 2000.

China's one-child policy has slowed population growth but has brought other problems. The Chinese traditionally love families and children, and the single child in many households is being badly spoiled – the Chinese call them "little emperors." Because boys are traditionally seen as better than girls, there are stories of girl babies being killed at birth.

Economic and political change

China's new economic freedom has resulted in one of the fastest growing economies in the world. The Chinese have more money and opportunities than ever before, and are looking beyond China's boundaries both for new things to buy and for new ideas. Although the Communist Party has allowed economic changes, there are now calls for political changes. In 1989 thousands demonstrated in Beijing against the lack of political freedom in China. They were suppressed by the army, and for the moment government change seems unlikely.

Modern Chinese couples like to have their picture taken dressed in western-style wedding clothes. Wedding gifts are piled high to display their wealth.

Regional differences

Another concern is the growing differences between areas of China. In towns and cities people have television sets and modern clothes, whereas for the majority in the countryside life is simple and relatively poor. The west of China and other remote areas are especially backward compared with the rich, densely populated eastern areas. This is adding to the unrest in some border regions where some non-Chinese want to be free of Chinese control.

The Chinese government believes such a large country needs strong central rule and that controls on people's freedom are necessary. Their strict policies of the past are gradually changing, allowing the Chinese to make the most out of their land and other raw materials. China is rich in resources and its people are hard-working – it could well become a wealthy and powerful country in the future.

Life for the majority of Chinese who live in the countryside has improved dramatically over the past 50 years, although most still work long hard hours in the fields.

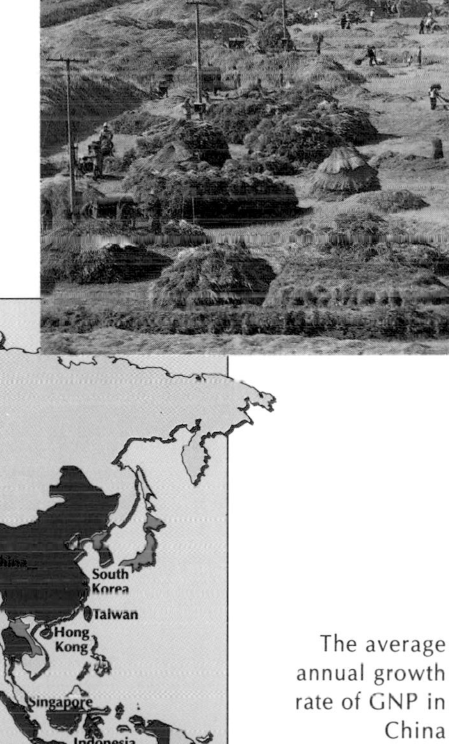

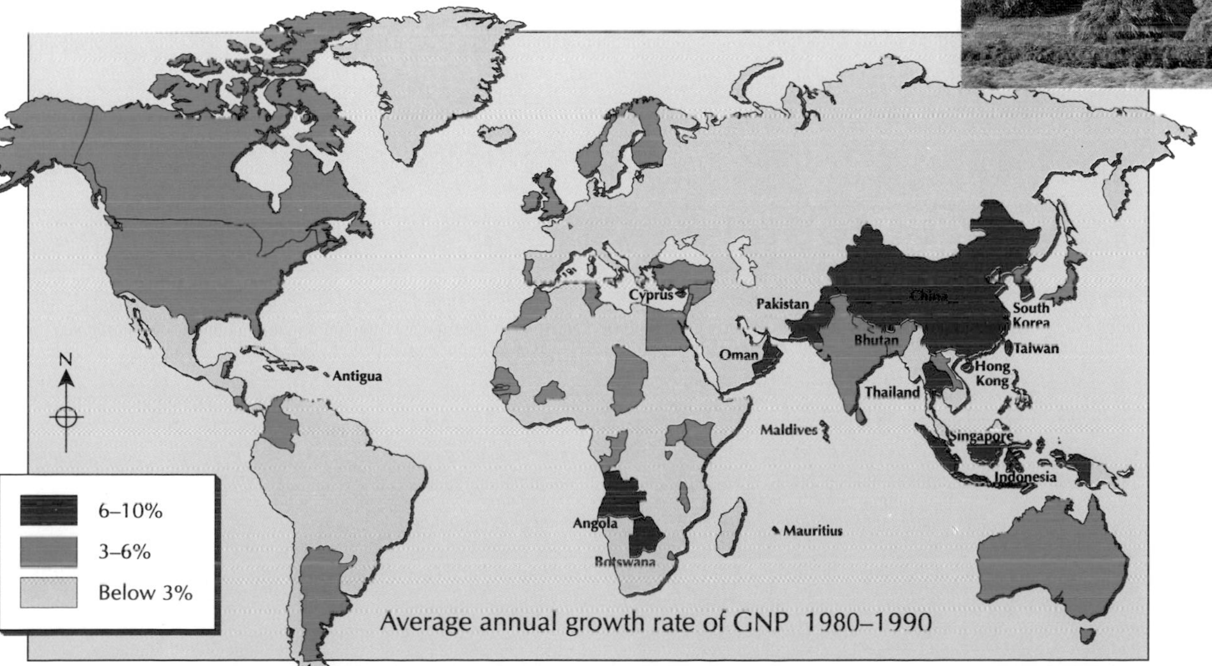

The average annual growth rate of GNP in China compared with the rest of the world.

Databank

The country

- Official name is The People's Republic of China.
- The total area of China is 3,695,500 sq mi (9,751,300 sq km).
- The capital city is Beijing.

Population

- The total population, based on a 1991 official estimate, is 1,158,230,000. It is estimated this will rise to 1,300,000,000 by the year 2000.
- The population of the three largest cities is:
  Shanghai 7,830,000
  Beijing 7,000,000
  Tianjin 5,770,000
- The urban population makes up about 26 percent of the total. (The urban population is 76 percent in the United States, 90 percent in the UK, and 28 percent in India.)

Physical geography

- China's longest river is the Yangtze (called Chang Jiang in Chinese). It is 3,915 mi (6,300 km) long. The Yellow River (called Huang He in Chinese) is 2,903 mi (4,672 km) long.
- The highest mountain is Mount Qomolangma (Mount Everest), 29,028 ft (8,848 m).
- The largest lake is Qinghai Lake (1,769 sq mi/4,584 sq km). It is a salt lake.
- China has no time zones. Even though the country is so large, it is all run on Beijing time. So at 8 o'clock in the morning when it is light in Beijing, it may still be dark in the west of the country.

Climate

	Lhasa	Beijing	Chengdu	Guangzhou
Average rainfall (yr)	24 inches (610 mm)	27 inches (700 mm)	43 inches (1125 mm)	65 inches (1618 mm)
Average monthly temperature				
January	28.4°F (–2°C)	23°F (–5°C)	43°F (6°C)	57°F (14°C)
July	59°F (15°C)	81°F (27°C)	77°F (25°C)	84°F (29°C)

Languages

- The official language taught at school and spoken on TV is Mandarin Chinese. Its official name is Putonghua.
- There are also several regional and local dialects, e.g. Tibetan, Cantonese, Wu, Xiang, Uyghur.
- It will help you to read the Chinese words in this book if you know that:
  "x" is pronounced like "sh," as in "she"
  "q" is pronounced like "ch," as in "cheek"
  "zh" is pronounced like "j," as in "jump"

The economy

- The unit of currency is the yuan. It is commonly known as "renminbi," which means "people's currency."
- The GNP (Gross National Product) of China in 1991 was $424,012 million. (In the UK it was $963,696 million, and in the United States it was $5,686,038 million.)
- China has one of the highest growth rates in the world. In 1991 the GNP grew by about 7 percent, which is more than double the economic growth rate of countries like the UK and the United States.

Life expectancy

- Changes in average life expectancy at birth in China between 1950 and 1995:
  1950–55 40 years old
  1970–75 63 years old
  1990–95 70 years old

Customs

- Few Chinese can take vacations where and when they want. Often a work unit will organize a group trip, by train or bus, to go and visit a famous sight. Other vacations are spent with the family.
- Chinese characters in the old days used to be written from the top of the page down to the bottom. Today they are usually written from left to right.
- Before the Republic of China was founded in 1912, some girls had their feet bound so that they could not grow properly. Small feet were considered pretty, but the girls with bound feet could hardly walk.
- The Chinese always have their soup near the end of their meal, not at the beginning.

Glossary

altitude
The height of land (or an object) above sea level.

Buddhist
A follower of the world religion called Buddhism. Buddha was a holy man from India.

Christian
A person who follows the teachings of Jesus Christ.

communist
A follower of the political idea that everything should be owned and controlled by the community and shared by everyone.

cultivate
To prepare land and to grow crops.

democratic
Describes a government that is elected or chosen by all the people.

drought
A long period without any rain.

dynasty
A long line of rulers from the same family.

eroded
Worn away.

exploit
To take advantage or make use of something.

fertile
Describes soil in which crops and other plants grow well.

Gross National Product (GNP)
The total value of everything produced by a country, plus its foreign income earnings.

human rights
Freedom and justice to which everyone is entitled.

hydroelectricity
Electricity which is made using the power of moving water.

irrigation
Watering the land with the help of specially built canals, pipes, etc.

loess
A fine yellowish-brown soil.

methane
A gas that burns easily.

monsoon
A wind that blows from the northeast in winter and from the southwest in summer, when it brings heavy rains to south Asian countries.

Muslim
Someone who follows the Islamic religion, founded by Muhammad.

nomads
People who have no settled home and move from place to place.

oasis
An area in the desert where there is water.

protein
A substance that people need to eat to survive. It is found in meat, cheese, milk, eggs, and beans.

reservoir
A natural or artificial lake in which water is stored.

self-sufficient
To be able to take care of oneself without help.

Silk Road
An ancient overland route between China and the west. Silk and other goods were taken along it by traders.

silt
Very fine pieces of soil and rock that are carried and deposited by a river.

smog
A smoky fog caused by pollution in the air.

solar power
Energy from the heat and/or the light of the sun.

Soviet Union
A group of republics that, before 1992, formed the Union of Soviet Socialist Republics under communist rule.

superstitious
Believing in or fearing, in an unreasonable way, the supernatural or the unknown.

terrain
Natural features of the surface of ground or land.

textile
A woven fabric.

uninhabitable
Describes a place where it is impossible to live.

urban
In or belonging to a town or city.

yak
A kind of hairy ox found in the mountains of Tibet.

Index

PRINTED IN BELGIUM BY proost INTERNATIONAL BOOK PRODUCTION